W9-AOZ-622

A Note to Parents and Caregivers:

Read-it! Readers are for children who are just starting on the amazing road to reading. These beautiful books support both the acquisition of reading skills and the love of books.

The PURPLE LEVEL presents basic topics and objects using high frequency words and simple language patterns.

The RED LEVEL presents familiar topics using common words and repeating sentence patterns.

The BLUE LEVEL presents new ideas using a larger vocabulary and varied sentence structure.

The YELLOW LEVEL presents more challenging ideas, a broad vocabulary, and wide variety in sentence structure.

The GREEN LEVEL presents more complex ideas, an extended vocabulary range, and expanded language structures.

The ORANGE LEVEL presents a wide range of ideas and concepts using challenging vocabulary and complex language structures.

When sharing a book with your child, read in short stretches, pausing often to talk about the pictures. Have your child turn the pages and point to the pictures and familiar words. And be sure to reread favorite stories or parts of stories.

There is no right or wrong way to share books with children. Find time to read with your child, and pass on the legacy of literacy.

Adria F. Klein, Ph.D.
Professor Emeritus
California State University
San Bernardino, California

Editor: Christianne Jones
Page Production: Brandie Shoemaker
Creative Director: Keith Griffin
Editorial Director: Carol Jones

First American edition published in 2007 by
Picture Window Books
5115 Excelsior Boulevard
Suite 232
Minneapolis, MN 55416
877-845-8392
www.picturewindowbooks.com

Copyright © 2004 by Allegra Publishing Limited
Unit 13/15 Quayside Lodge
William Morris Way
Townmead Road
London SW6 2UZ UK

Printed in the United States of America.

Library of Congress Cataloging-in-Publication Data
Law, Felicia.
Rumble meets Wilson Wolf / by Felicia Law ; illustrated by Yoon-Mi Pak.—1st
American ed.
p. cm. — (Read-it! readers)
Summary: Wilson Wolf checks into the honeymoon room at Rumble's Cave Hotel
and then demands that the proprietor find him a wife.
ISBN-13: 978-1-4048-1288-8 (hardcover)
ISBN-10: 1-4048-1288-1 (hardcover)
[1. Wolves—Fiction. 2. Hotels, motels, etc.—Fiction. 3. Dragons—Fiction.] I. Pak,
Yoon Mi, ill. II. Title. III. Series.

PZ7.L41835Rumy 2007
[E]—dc22   2006003412

Rumble Meets Wilson Wolf

by Felicia Law
illustrated by Yoon-Mi Pak

Special thanks to our advisers for their expertise:

Adria F. Klein, Ph.D.
Professor Emeritus, California State University
San Bernardino, California

Susan Kesselring, M.A.
Literacy Educator
Rosemount–Apple Valley–Eagan (Minnesota) School District

PiCTURE WiNDOW BOOKS
Minneapolis, Minnesota

This is the life of a cool, young dragon named Rumble. When his grandma leaves her run-down cave to him, Rumble sets about making it into a four-star hotel. He doesn't do it all alone. He has help from a picky hotel inspector and an annoying spider named Shelby.

Wilson Wolf has arrived at Rumble's Cave Hotel dressed for his wedding. But he doesn't have a bride! Instead, he asks Rumble to find him one. Will Rumble find a suitable wife for Wilson Wolf?

"Knock, knock," said Wilson Wolf, "is this Rumble's Cave Hotel?"

"Yes, it is," said Shelby Spider, who was busy polishing the hotel star.

8

"I've come to stay, and I want the best honeymoon room," said Wilson.

"Congratulations, sir," said Rumble. "Where's your wife?"

"I don't have a wife yet," said Wilson. "That's why I'm here. I want you to find me a wife."

"Oh, dear!" said Rumble. "I'm not sure we have a spare wife. We have a spare bedroom and a spare table for dinner, but we don't have any spare wives."

"Then," said Wilson as he climbed the stairs, "you will need to look for one."

11

"I have a wedding jacket. I have a flower in my buttonhole. I have a bag full of confetti. I am all ready for my wedding. I just need a wife," said Wilson.

"OK. I'll try to find you a wife," said Rumble with a sigh.

Wilson Wolf slammed his door shut and went to bed.

"He's snoring," said Rumble.

"That's a problem," said Shelby Spider. "No one will marry a wolf who snores."

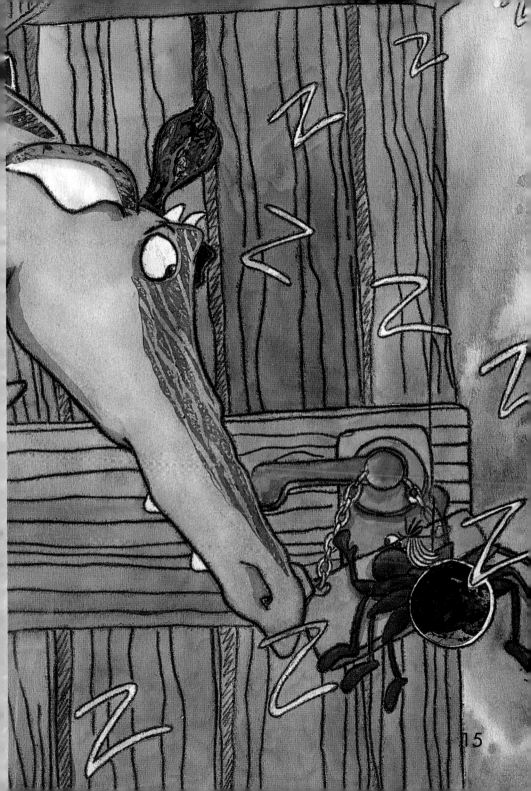

15

Wilson Wolf slept all day and all night.

The next morning, Milly the Maid knocked on the door.

"Housekeeping!" she called out loudly. "Can I come in?"

"Go away!" said Wilson Wolf.

At noon, Milly the Maid knocked on the door again.

"Housekeeping!" she called out loudly. "Can I come in?"

This time Wilson Wolf sprang out of bed. Maybe it was his wife.

"Come in," he said. "Are you my wife?"

"No, I'm the maid," said Milly. "I'm here to clean."

19

"I don't need a maid. I need a wife," said
Wilson Wolf.

"I think you do need a maid," Milly said
as she looked around. "Your room is
a mess."

"A wife who will clean is a better idea,"
said Wilson. "Perhaps I'll marry you."

"Don't be silly," Milly said. "A wolf can't
marry a chicken."

21

That day, Wilson ate a huge lunch. He ate five plates of roast meat, four plates of potatoes, three plates of bread pudding, two plates of ginger cookies, and a large dish of the Chef's Special—cold porridge.

At the end of the meal, there was no more food left in the kitchen.

23

"That wolf doesn't need a wife," said Chester the Chef. "He needs a servant who will buy his food, a chef who will cook his meals, and a maid who will clean up his mess."

"And someone to poke him when he snores," added Shelby Spider.

"Oh, dear," sighed Rumble. "He won't go until he's got a wife, but he's the worst guest ever!"

"I think Shelby should marry him," said Chester. "She doesn't have a husband, and he's clearly very rich."

"Good idea," said Rumble.

"I guess it wouldn't be that bad," said Shelby. "As long as we could do something about that snoring."

Wilson Wolf wasn't at all happy when Rumble told him the news.

"I want a wife," he growled, "not an ugly spider."

"Spiders make very good wives," said Rumble. "Shelby may be the best wife you can find."

"No way!" said Wilson Wolf. "I'm leaving!"

Wilson Wolf stomped off down the hill.

"I guess it wasn't so hard to get rid of him," said Rumble. "I'm sure he'll find a wife, and they'll live happily ever after."

"A wife who snores," smiled Shelby Spider.

31

MORE *Read-it!* READERS

Bright pictures and fun stories help you practice your reading skills. Look for more books at your level.

Happy Birthday, Gus! 1-4048-0957-0

Happy Easter, Gus! by 1-4048-0959-7

Happy Halloween, Gus! 1-4048-0960-0

Happy Thanksgiving, Gus! 1-4048-0961-9

Happy Valentine's Day, Gus! 1-4048-0962-7

Matt Goes to Mars 1-4048-1269-5

Merry Christmas, Gus! 1-4048-0958-9

Rumble Meets Buddy Beaver 1-4048-1287-3

Rumble Meets Chester the Chef 1-4048-1335-7

Rumble Meets Eli Elephant 1-4048-1332-2

Rumble Meets Keesha Kangaroo 1-4048-1290-3

Rumble Meets Milly the Maid by 1-4048-1341-1

Rumble Meets Penny Panther by 1-4048-1331-4

Rumble Meets Sylvia and Sally Swan by 1-4048-1541-4

Rumble Meets Wally Warthog 1-4048-1289-X

Looking for a specific title or level? A complete list of *Read-it!* Readers is available on our Web site: **www.picturewindowbooks.com**